MATH ADVENTURES

STELLA SELLS LEMONADE

A SUBTRACTION ADVENTURE

by Megan Atwood
illustrated by Amy Zhing

GRASSHOPPER

Tools for Parents & Teachers

Grasshopper Books enhance imagination and introduce the earliest readers to fiction with fun storylines and illustrations. The easy-to-read text supports early reading experiences with repetitive sentence patterns and sight words.

Before Reading

- Look at the cover illustration. What do readers see? What do they think the book will be about?
- Look at the picture glossary together. Sound out the words. Ask readers to identify the first letter of each vocabulary word.

Read the Book

- "Walk" through the book, reading to or along with the reader. Point to the illustrations as you read.

After Reading

- Review the picture glossary again. Ask readers to locate the words in the text.
- Ask the reader: Stella subtracts each time someone buys a cup of lemonade. What have you subtracted today?

Grasshopper Books are published by Jump!
5357 Penn Avenue South
Minneapolis, MN 55419
www.jumplibrary.com

Library of Congress Cataloging-in-Publication Data

Names: Atwood, Megan, author. | Zhing, Amy, illustrator.
Title: Stella sells lemonade: a subtraction adventure by Megan Atwood; illustrated by Amy Zhing.
Description: Minneapolis, MN: Jump!, Inc., [2022]
Series: Math adventures
Audience: Ages 4-7.
Identifiers: LCCN 2021038091 (print)
LCCN 2021038092 (ebook)
ISBN 9781636906355 (hardcover)
ISBN 9781636906362 (paperback)
ISBN 9781636906379 (ebook)
Subjects: LCSH: Readers (Primary)
Subtraction–Juvenile fiction.
LCGFT: Readers (Publications)
Classification: LCC PE1119.2 .A897 2022 (print)
LCC PE1119.2 (ebook) | DDC 428.6/2–dc23
LC record available at https://lccn.loc.gov/2021038091
LC ebook record available at https://lccn.loc.gov/2021038092

Editor: Eliza Leahy
Direction and Layout: Anna Peterson
Illustrator: Amy Zhing

Printed in the United States of America at Corporate Graphics in North Mankato, Minnesota.

Table of Contents

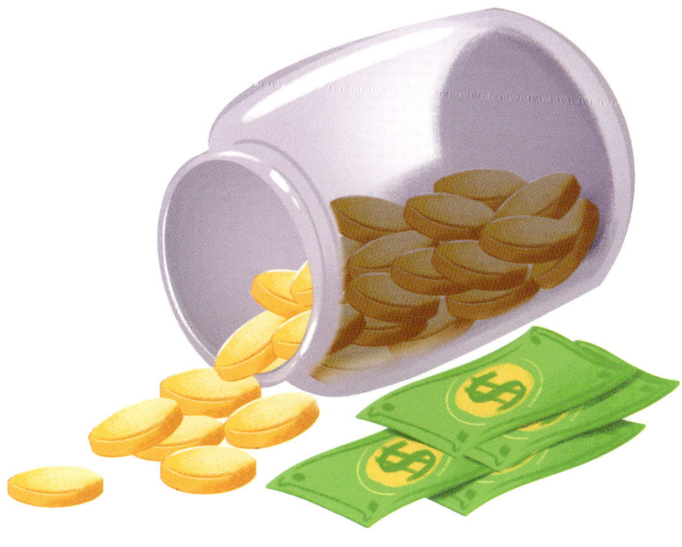

Buying and Selling

"I'm going to sell lemonade!" says Stella.

She counts seven lemons.

She needs four lemons to make juice.

That leaves three lemons.

"Can I have these?" Stella's brother asks.

"Sure, Max!" she says.

Max takes the three lemons.

Stella sets up her stand.

She has ten cups to sell.

But Max took two!

Now she only has eight.

LEMONADE
LEMONADE
50¢

Stella's neighbor buys three cups.

Stella has five cups left.

LEMONADE
8 – 3 = 5

Stella sells two more cups.

Now she has three cups left.

Stella's friend stops by.

She buys one cup.

"I still have two cups,"
says Stella.

"I'll buy them!" says Max.

One for him. One for Stella.

"Thank you, Max!"
Stella says.

2 - 2 = 0

Let's Review!

Stella's brother, Max, appears throughout the story. How many times do you see Max in the book?

A. one time **B.** five times **C.** six times **D.** ten times

Picture Glossary

buys
Gets something for paying money.

lemonade
A drink made of lemon juice, water, and sugar.

lemons
Yellow citrus fruits with thick skin and a sour taste.

sell
To give something and receive money back.

Let's Review! Answer Key: **B.** five times